Leah
the Theatre
Fairy

Beatrice Rose carington

Special thanks to
Narinder Dhami

ORCHARD BOOKS

First published in Great Britain in 2011 by Orchard Books
This edition published in 2018 by The Watts Publishing Group

1 3 5 7 9 10 8 6 4 2

Copyright © 2018 Rainbow Magic Limited.
Copyright © 2018 HIT Entertainment Limited.
Illustrations copyright © Orchard Books 2011

HIT entertainment

A CIP catalogue record for this book is available from the British Library.

ISBN 978 1 40835 898 6

Printed in Great Britain by Clays Ltd, Elcograf S.p.A.

MIX
Paper from
responsible sources
FSC® C104740

The paper and board used in this book are made from wood from responsible sources

Orchard Books
An imprint of Hachette Children's Group
Part of The Watts Publishing Group Limited
Carmelite House, 50 Victoria Embankment, London EC4Y 0DZ

An Hachette UK Company
www.hachette.co.uk
www.hachettechildrens.co.uk

Leah
the Theatre
Fairy

by Daisy Meadows

Join the **Rainbow Magic Reading Challenge!**

Read the story and collect your fairy points to climb the Reading Rainbow at the back of the book.

This book is worth 5 points.

Who likes talent shows? Not me!
So, goblins, listen carefully,
Each Showtime Fairy has a star,
Their magic glitters near and far.

Now do exactly as I say,
And steal these magical stars away,
Then, when our wicked work is done,
We can spoil all showtime fun!

Contents

A Grand Old Theatre

"Oh, this is amazing!" Kirsty exclaimed. She stared out of the car window at the grand old theatre with its carved mahogany doors, mirrored glass and ornate, old-fashioned lamps hanging outside. There was a painted sign over the entrance with 'The Swan Theatre' written in golden letters. "I can't wait to see inside."

"It's really beautiful, Kirsty," Rachel said as her mum stopped the car. "The theatre's Victorian, and it still looks just like it did in the olden days!"

"I saw the pantomime *Aladdin* here last Christmas," Zac added. He was one of Rachel's school friends. "It was brilliant."

"Thank you for the lift, Mrs Walker," said Tanya, another of Rachel's friends.

"I hope the rehearsal goes well," Mrs Walker said, "I'll pick you all up in a couple of hours."

Rachel, Kirsty, Zac and Tanya jumped out of the car. The Swan Theatre was just outside Tippington town, and it was too far for them to walk there. That was probably why she'd never seen the theatre when she'd stayed with Rachel before, Kirsty thought.

"I'm really glad you invited me for half-term, Rachel," Kirsty said happily as the four of them went up the marble steps to the entrance doors.

The leaves on the trees outside the theatre were turning red, gold and orange, and there was an autumn chill in the air. "It's so exciting to be here for all the auditions *and* for the Variety Show at the end of the week!"

Rachel nodded. Every day during half-term, the Tippington Variety Show organisers were holding auditions for local schools in magic, drama, acrobatics, dance, singing and ice skating, and the winning acts would be performing in the Variety Show. The money raised by the show would be used to pay for an adventure playground, a bandstand *and* an outdoor theatre in Tippington's Oval Park!

"It'll be fun putting on a play in a real theatre, won't it?" Rachel remarked.

Tonight the drama auditions were being held at The Swan Theatre, and each school was performing a short play based on a fairytale. Tippington School were doing *Cinderella*, and Rachel had helped to write the script.

"Yes, but I can't help feeling a bit nervous," Tanya admitted. She was playing the part of the Fairy Godmother and Zac was in charge of the lighting.

"You'll be fine!" Kirsty told her.

"Didn't Holly do well yesterday?" Zac said, pulling open the entrance door. "She's a fantastic magician."

13

Holly, another friend from Tippington School, had won the first audition and would be performing her magic act in the Variety Show.

"Yes, Holly was great," Rachel agreed. She caught Kirsty's eye and the two of them shared a secret smile. Holly wasn't the only person who knew a lot about magic, Rachel thought! And now she and Kirsty were right in the middle of another thrilling fairy adventure…

Yesterday at the magic auditions, Madison the Magic Show Fairy had introduced herself to the girls and then whisked them off to Fairyland to meet the other Showtime Fairies. The Showtime Fairies each had a special star on the tip of their wands, and with these magical stars they made sure that everyone in both the human and the fairy worlds could use their showtime talents and skills to the full. But while the Showtime Fairies and some of their friends had been rehearsing for their very own Variety Show, grumpy Jack Frost had decided to put a stop to all the fun. He'd sent his goblins to steal the Showtime Fairies' magical stars and hide them away in the human world. The missing stars meant that everyone, both humans and fairies, had now lost their showtime skills. The magic show auditions yesterday had almost been ruined, but Rachel and Kirsty had managed to find Madison's star and get it back from the goblins just in time.

"Can you believe the cheek of those goblins yesterday, Rachel?" Kirsty murmured as Tanya and Zac went on ahead of them.

"Imagine pretending to be from a school called Icy Towers and taking part in the magic show auditions!"

"Let's hope they don't try to spoil the drama auditions today, too," Rachel said anxiously.

"But the auditions won't go well anyway, unless we find Leah the Theatre Fairy's star," Kirsty reminded her.

The foyer of The Swan Theatre was beautifully decorated in red and gold with sweeping marble staircases on either side leading up to the balcony seats. Miss Patel, the teacher who was organising the Tippington School auditions, was near the box office talking with the rest of the cast. Rachel, Kirsty, Zac and Tanya went to join them.

"Ah, there you are!" Miss Patel smiled at them. "Rachel, did you bring your script?" Rachel nodded and held up her clipboard.

"Good," Miss Patel went on, "You'll be sitting at the side of the stage to remind anyone who forgets their lines!"

"OK, Miss Patel," Rachel replied. "And Kirsty was wondering if she could help, too."

"Maybe I could look after the props," Kirsty suggested.

"That's an excellent idea, Kirsty," Miss Patel said gratefully. "I was going to sort out the props myself, but I have so many other things to do! They're all laid out backstage, so there isn't much to do until the dress rehearsal actually starts."

She clapped her hands. "Right, all the actors go backstage and get changed into your costumes, please. And Zac, you'd better check the lighting."

Tanya and the other actors headed off to the dressing-rooms, while Zac took the stairs to the lighting booth.

"Kirsty and I have some free time until the rehearsal begins," Rachel said to Miss Patel. "Could we have a look around the theatre?"

"Of course," Miss Patel agreed.

Rachel led Kirsty down a corridor lined
with a red carpet woven with gold stars.
At the end of the corridor was
a set of wooden doors, and
Rachel pushed them open.

"Oh!" Kirsty gasped
as they walked into
the theatre itself.
"You were right,
Rachel. This is
beautiful!"

The Victorian
theatre hadn't
changed much at
all over the years. It
was like stepping back
in time, Kirsty thought.
Everything was decorated
luxuriously in the same

colours as the foyer. The seats were red velvet trimmed with gold braid, and the heavy stage curtains, which were drawn back at the moment, were also red and gold. There were ornate, carved trails of flowers climbing the walls, and the old gas lamps were still in place. The sweeping, curved balcony above their heads was also decorated with gilt carvings, as were the boxes on either side of the stage, and a crystal chandelier hung from the ceiling.

"It's a magical place, isn't it?" Rachel said as she and Kirsty walked down one of the aisles between the rows of seats. "Maybe we'll see some fairy magic here today."

"And we'd better be on the lookout for those naughty goblins, too!" Kirsty added.

As the girls wandered further down the aisle, Rachel frowned. She had just noticed a tiny spotlight shimmering brightly, right in the middle of the stage.

"I wonder what that is, Kirsty?" Rachel remarked, pointing it out to her friend.

"Maybe it's Zac checking the lights," Kirsty suggested.

"But I'm sure that spotlight isn't coming from the lighting booth." Rachel peered upwards, shading her eyes. "Look, it's shining down from that box up there!"

Suddenly the light drifted out of the box above their heads and headed straight down towards them. As the beam came closer, Kirsty let out a gasp of delight. "It's Leah the Theatre Fairy!" she cried.

All in a Muddle

"Hello, girls!" Leah called with a smile.

The fairy flew down lower, her long, dark hair floating out behind her. It was caught up on one side of her head with a sparkly clip. Leah's strapless dress with its full underskirts billowed out as she hovered in the air in front of Rachel and Kirsty.

"We were hoping we'd see you, Leah," said Rachel. "Our school is about to start rehearsing for the drama audition."

Leah glanced sadly at her empty wand. "And nothing will go right for anyone until I get my magical star back," she sighed.

"What does your star look like, Leah?" asked Kirsty.

"It shimmers with rainbow colours and it has a picture on it of two masks, one happy and one sad," Leah explained. "They show the two sides of drama — comedy and tragedy."

"And do you think the missing star is somewhere in the theatre?" Rachel wanted to know.

Leah nodded. "I'm sure of it," she replied. "And if we don't find it before the drama auditions tonight, they'll be ruined!"

Just then they heard the sound of footsteps and people talking backstage.

"Miss Patel and the others are coming," Rachel said. "You'd better hide, Leah!"

Quickly Leah fluttered out of sight under a page of Rachel's script as Miss Patel and the cast came out onto the stage.

"Right, let's begin," Miss Patel called. "Rachel, there's a chair ready for you. And, Kirsty, here's a list of the props."

Rachel sat down in the wings, holding her script carefully so that no-one could see Leah beneath the pages. The props were also waiting in the wings, and Kirsty checked them off the list. They included a pumpkin, a broom and a pair of pretty glass slippers with pink bows.

The dress rehearsal began. Kirsty, Rachel and Leah watched as the invitation for Prince Charming's ball arrived. Cinderella's ugly stepsisters were very excited, but they were determined not to allow Cinderella to go to the ball, too.

"WE WON'T TELL CINDERELLA THAT HER NAME'S ON THE INVITATION, TOO!" shouted the first ugly stepsister at the top of her voice.

"SHE CAN STAY AT HOME AND CLEAN THE HOUSE, HA HA!" yelled the other stepsister.

Surprised, Rachel glanced down at her script. That wasn't what was written at all. The ugly stepsisters were supposed to whisper those lines to each other, not shout them!

The stepsisters told Cinderella that she wasn't invited to the ball. Cinderella was supposed to look very sad at this point, but suddenly Violet, the girl who was playing her, burst into giggles. Rachel shook her head in dismay. That wasn't in the script either!

"Sorry, Miss Patel," Violet said, looking rather embarrassed. "I don't know what got into me!"

"We're all getting in a muddle," added one of the ugly stepsisters.

"We know what's going on, don't we,

Rachel?" Kirsty murmured. "This is all down to Leah's missing star!"

Looking upset, Rachel nodded. Things went from bad to worse after that. The ugly stepsisters headed off to the ball, and Cinderella was left at home to clean the kitchen. Kirsty had the broom ready in the wings. But Violet had just begun to sweep the stage when the broom handle snapped in two. Zac couldn't get the lights working properly and kept spotlighting the wrong people.

Then, when Kirsty picked up the glass slippers, the bows fell off.

"Everything's going wrong today!" said Miss Patel with a sigh.

Suddenly there was a crash as the door in the shadows at the back of the theatre swung open. Everyone, including Rachel, Kirsty and Leah, jumped.

A schoolboy in a bright green blazer with a matching cap pulled right down over his face marched in. He was carrying a tray in front of him. "Ice cream!" he called in a loud voice. "Get your ice cream here!"

Four other boys wearing the same uniform rushed in after him.

"I want ice cream!" one yelled.

"Me first!" shouted another.

As the boys scuffled with each other, trying to grab the ice cream, Rachel turned to Kirsty.

"Goblins!" she whispered.

Celebrity Goblins!

"Excuse me, boys," Miss Patel called to the goblins from the front of the theatre, "But you shouldn't be eating ice cream until the interval tonight. You're interrupting our rehearsal. And what are you doing here anyway? Do you have a rehearsal booked?"

The goblins began winking at each other and grinning very smugly.

"Icy Towers doesn't need to rehearse!" one of them scoffed.

"We're just naturally brilliant!" another boasted.

Rachel and Kirsty glanced at each other.

"It sounds like the goblins have the magic star with them," Kirsty whispered. "That's why they're so confident."

The goblins skipped down the aisle, jumped on stage and then disappeared into the wings. Rachel and Kirsty watched them head backstage, still clutching their ice creams.

"We've got to follow them," Rachel said in a low voice.

Kirsty nodded. "Miss Patel, Rachel and I are going to try and fix the broom and the slippers," she said.

"Good idea," Miss Patel agreed. "Let's take a short break. Maybe then things will start to go right again!"

Kirsty grabbed the two halves of the broom handle and Rachel picked up the glass slippers. As she did so, Leah slipped out of the pages of the script and hid herself inside one of the slippers.

"Quick, girls, find somewhere to hide!" Leah murmured. "Then I can mend the props with my magic, and we can fly after the goblins!"

Rachel and Kirsty slipped behind a painted backdrop of a castle. Immediately Leah fluttered out of the slipper, tapping it with her wand as she did so. A few sparkles of fairy magic fixed the bows back in place, and another wave of Leah's wand stuck the two halves of the broom handle firmly together.

"And now for the goblins!" Leah said with a wink. She pointed her wand at the girls and a puff of magical fairy dust surrounded them. In an instant Rachel and Kirsty were fairy-sized like Leah, with shimmering wings on their backs!

The three friends flew along the
corridor until they found the goblins
in one of the dressing-rooms. The
door was ajar and Leah,
Rachel and Kirsty
peeped in.

The goblins were
sitting in plush,
comfy chairs in
front of make-
up mirrors edged
with glowing
lightbulbs.
They'd taken off
their blazers and slung
them over the backs of
the chairs. Now they were
opening up boxes of stage make-up
and checking what was inside.

Silently Leah pointed at a rack of costumes in a corner of the room. Kirsty and Rachel nodded. The three of them slipped unnoticed through the door and hid behind a purple velvet cloak hanging on the rack.

The goblins were now trying out the stage make-up. They were smearing pink blusher on their cheeks and powdering their long noses. Rachel bit her lip, trying not to laugh.

"I look like a star now," one of the goblins said dreamily, eyeing his reflection in the mirror with great satisfaction.

"Remember what Jack Frost said," one of the others reminded him.

"Of course I remember!" the first goblin said crossly. Then he looked a bit sheepish. "Er – what did Jack Frost say?" he mumbled.

"He said we had to use the magic star to ruin the auditions," the second goblin replied. "Not to become stars ourselves."

"Well, why can't we do both?" the first goblin demanded sulkily as he rooted through the make-up box again. "It's not fair. I want to be famous!"

The other goblins snorted with laughter.

"You're too ugly to be famous!" one of them said with a snigger. The first goblin was so annoyed, he threw a powder puff at him.

Leah turned to Rachel and Kirsty. "Let's look for the star while the goblins are busy putting on their stage make-up!" she said. "But be very careful they don't see you."

Pumpkins or Cabbages?

As the goblins began applying sparkly eye shadow, Leah, Kirsty and Rachel flew out from behind the costumes. Keeping low down so that the goblins didn't spot them in the mirrors, they began searching the blazers hanging on the backs of the chairs.

Leah and the girls checked all the pockets one by one, but to their dismay, there was no sign of the star.

"Maybe I'll win an award for Best Actor," the first goblin said hopefully, preening himself in the mirror. Kirsty had to try very hard not to burst out laughing.

Suddenly a voice echoed down the corridor. "Rachel! Kirsty! Where are you?"

"That's Miss Patel," Rachel whispered to Leah. "We'd better go."

Leah nodded. "My star's not here anyway," she sighed. "Where *have* the goblins hidden it?"

Kirsty, Rachel and Leah quickly
zoomed out of the dressing-room and
back towards the stage. They hid behind
the painted backdrop once more, and
Leah's magic made Rachel and Kirsty
human-sized again. Leah fluttered
down to hide behind
Rachel's hair, and
then, carrying
the broom
and slippers,
the girls
hurried to
join Miss
Patel and
the others.

"Ah, there
you are,"
Miss Patel said.

"And you've managed to mend the props – wonderful!" She examined the broom and slippers, then beamed with delight. "You'd never even know they were broken!"

Rachel and Kirsty grinned at each other. Fairy magic was brilliant!

"Right, let's do a final run-through," Miss Patel called. "Rachel, will you prompt again, please?"

Rachel nodded and went back into the wings with Kirsty. Then the girls saw Leah flutter off Rachel's shoulder and quietly fly up to perch on top of the scenery.

The play began, but things weren't much better than before.

No-one could remember their lines, and
Rachel kept having to prompt them.
Then, when they got to the scene where
the Fairy Godmother appeared, Tanya
walked on stage, tripped over the hem
of her long flowing dress
and tore a hole in it.

"You shall
go to the ball,
Cinderella!"
Tanya
declared,
trying to ignore
her ripped dress.
"Bring me a pumpkin!"

"The pumpkin's vanished!" Kirsty
gasped, sorting frantically through
the props. "Where's it gone? It was here
a moment ago."

"This is all because Leah's star is missing!" Rachel groaned.

"Just carry on without the pumpkin," called Miss Patel.

Tanya waved her wand. Immediately Zac dimmed the lights and there was a moment of darkness. Rachel knew this was so that the pupils in charge of the scenery could wheel Cinderella's coach onto the stage.

The lights went up again, and there was the coach, made from gold-painted cardboard. But the coach wasn't the only thing that had appeared while the lights were dimmed. Standing on the stage there was another Cinderella, another pair of ugly stepsisters, another Fairy Godmother and another Prince Charming.

Rachel and Kirsty both gasped with horror. Underneath the stage make-up they could see the imposters were goblins! They had obviously dressed themselves up in the costumes hanging on the rack in the dressing-room.

Now the goblin godmother stepped forward. He wore a long, frilly dress and a sparkling tiara, and he held a wand in his hand.

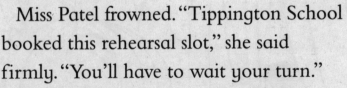

"It's time for Icy Towers to take over the stage!" the goblin godmother announced.

Miss Patel frowned. "Tippington School booked this rehearsal slot," she said firmly. "You'll have to wait your turn."

The goblin godmother scowled and pointed his wand at Miss Patel. "I'll turn everyone from Tippington School into pumpkins unless you let Icy Towers take over the stage right now!" he threatened.

The goblin Cinderella giggled. "Let's turn them into cabbages!" he suggested.

"No, Brussels sprouts!" one of the goblin stepsisters laughed.

Kirsty stared at the star on the tip of the goblin godmother's wand. It was shimmering with rainbow colours in the lights, but Kirsty was sure she could see something more. She edged out of the wings and onto the stage for a closer look. Now Kirsty could see two masks etched on the star, one happy, one sad.

"The goblin godmother has Leah's star!" Kirsty whispered.

Rachel turned pale. "Then we have to get it back — and fast!" she replied. "Now Leah's star is on the stage, it will give the goblins magical powers. And that means they might really use Leah's magic to turn everyone into vegetables!"

Who's the Star?

"This is wasting our time and yours," Miss Patel said, looking very annoyed with the goblins. "I'll call the organisers to sort out this mix-up."

Miss Patel walked off the stage, followed by the Tippington cast and crew. Rachel and Kirsty stayed behind, trying to think of a plan to get the star away from the goblins. A moment later Leah flitted down to join them.

"I see you spotted my star on the goblin godmother's wand!" Leah whispered. "The question is, how are we going to get it back?"

"Oh!" Kirsty exclaimed. "I think I have an idea!" And she began to explain her plan to Rachel and Leah in a low voice.

The goblins were now arguing with each other as to which of them was the star of the show.

"It's me, of course!" the Cinderella goblin said importantly. "The clue's in the title of the show – *Cinderella*!"

"There wouldn't be any show without me," the goblin godmother grumbled. "It's my magic that helps Cinderella go to the ball."

"Hello there," Kirsty called. She stepped out of the wings onto the stage.

56

"Shouldn't you be getting on with your rehearsal? Where's your script?"

The goblins hooted with laughter.

"We don't need a script," said the goblin Prince Charming. "We're stars!"

"Even stars need a script to act properly," Kirsty explained.

Waving her clipboard, Rachel also stepped out onto the stage. "I can direct you from my script," she offered.

"OK, let's get on with it then," the goblin Cinderella said rudely. "You shouldn't keep a star like me waiting!"

"Let's practise the scene where the Fairy Godmother tells Cinderella she has to be home by midnight," Kirsty suggested.

"But we're not in that scene!" the ugly stepsister goblins grumbled loudly.

"Neither am I," the goblin Prince

Charming muttered, looking
very put out.

"We'll practise your
scenes next,"
Kirsty told
them. Still
complaining,
the goblin
stepsisters
and prince
moved
reluctantly
to the back
of the stage.
Meanwhile,
Kirsty glanced
at Leah, and the
two of them slipped
away out of sight.

"Let's begin," Rachel called. "Cinderella, your first line is 'Thank you for my beautiful dress and the golden coach, Fairy Godmother. Now I can go to the ball!'"

The goblin Cinderella stepped forward, elbowing the goblin godmother out of the way.

"Thank you for my beautiful dress and the golden coach, Fairy Godmother," the goblin Cinderella said in a squeaky, high-pitched voice.

"Now I can go to the ball!"

"Fairy Godmother," Rachel went on,
"Your reply is 'You're welcome, my dear.
But you must be home by midnight or
your dress will turn to
rags, and your coach
will turn back into
a pumpkin again!'"

The goblin
Fairy Godmother
shoved the goblin
Cinderella out of the
way, took
centre stage and repeated Rachel's words.

"And now, Fairy Godmother," said
Rachel, "your last line is 'Goodbye and
good luck!' And when you say that, you
must toss your wand high above your
head into the air."

When the goblin looked a bit surprised, Rachel added quickly, "It's a special trick that'll make you the star of the show!"

The goblin Fairy Godmother looked delighted. He cleared his throat.

"Goodbye and good luck!" he screeched, preparing to throw his wand with the magic star up into the air.

Rachel held her breath.

"STOP!" yelled the goblin prince and one of the goblin stepsisters.

"Why?" asked the goblin Fairy
Godmother crossly. He was still clutching
the wand. "You just don't want me to be
the star of the show!"

"Look!" The goblin prince pointed
at Kirsty, who was hiding behind the
scenery. Meanwhile, the goblin stepsister
was glaring up at Leah who was perched
on top of the scenery. Both Leah and
Kirsty were ready and waiting to catch
the wand and retrieve the magic star.

"They're trying to
trick us!" shouted the
goblin Cinderella.

Kirsty exchanged
dismayed looks with
Leah and Rachel.
The goblins had
foiled their plan!

It's Showtime!

Rachel's heart sank. Dropping her clipboard, she slipped away to hide behind the curtain. Kirsty hurried after her and a moment later Leah flew down to join them.

"What now?" asked Kirsty anxiously. The goblins were still onstage, and Leah and the girls could hear them arguing yet again about who was the star of the show.

Rachel looked thoughtful. "The goblins want to be stars, don't they?" she said. "And stars need lots of really dazzling spotlights!"

Leah and Kirsty grinned as they realised exactly what Rachel meant.

"Let's go for it!" Leah whispered. She pointed her wand at the girls and a cloud of fairy sparkles shrank them down to fairy-size.

Then Kirsty fluttered up into the air, heading for the lighting booth at the back of the theatre. Meanwhile, Rachel and Leah flew back into the wings.

Kirsty whizzed into the lighting booth. She found the switches labelled 'spotlights' and began to flick them on and off. As she did so, bright beams of light flooded the stage briefly and then disappeared, only to reappear elsewhere.

"Ooh, that big spotlight must be for me, because I'm the star of the show!" shouted the goblin Fairy Godmother. Quickly Kirsty turned the spotlight off and on again, and the goblin was completely dazzled. He lurched forward and bumped straight into the goblin prince.

"Help!' shouted one of the goblin stepsisters. Kirsty had just flicked another spotlight on and off and then on again. "I can't see!" Covering his eyes, the goblin stepsister ran off across the stage, colliding with the golden coach.

"These lights are too bright!" grumbled the goblin prince. He stumbled backwards, trying to get away from a flickering spotlight, and fell over Cinderella's broom.

"I don't want to be a star any more!"

"Come on, Rachel!" Leah whispered in the wings.

The goblins were now blundering around the stage in total confusion, crashing into the scenery as well as each other. Staying in the wings so that they weren't dazzled by the spotlights themselves, Leah and Rachel zoomed towards the goblin Fairy Godmother.

They could see the magical star with its comedy and tragedy masks shimmering even more beautifully in the lights.

The goblin Fairy Godmother was backing away from a particularly bright spotlight, still clutching the wand.

"Stop it!" he yelled angrily, "You're dazzling us!" And he raised the wand high above his head, pointing it at Kirsty in the lighting booth.

"NOW!" Leah whispered.

She and Rachel swooped down on either side of the star. They each took hold of one of the points and lifted it gently off the goblin godmother's wand.

As soon as Leah touched the glittering star, it shrank right down to its fairy size. Leah slipped the star back on to her own wand where it glowed brightly with fairy magic, and the girls cheered.

"What's happened?" shrieked the goblin Fairy Godmother. He stared in disbelief at his empty wand. "My magical star's gone!"

"Yes, and that means the drama auditions won't be ruined tonight after all!" Kirsty told him, flying down from the lighting booth to join Rachel and Leah.

The goblins looked furious.

"Jack Frost is going to be really angry with us," muttered the goblin Cinderella as they slunk away. He glared at the goblin godmother. "This is all your fault.

You lost the star because you wanted to *be* a star!"

"Ooh, I did not!" shouted the goblin godmother crossly. "It was you! You're the one who kept going on about being a star!"

Complaining loudly, the goblins stomped out of the theatre via the backstage door.

"Thank you, girls," Leah laughed, waving her wand and returning the girls to human-size. "You two are the real stars! You've helped me save the auditions from disaster."

"We're so glad we could help," Rachel told her.

"I must go straight back to Fairyland and give them the wonderful news," Leah said happily. "Good luck tonight, girls – and don't give up searching until all the Showtime Fairies have their magical stars back!"

"We won't!" Kirsty promised as Leah vanished in a mist of fairy sparkles.

That evening, after the drama auditions were over, Kirsty and Rachel joined the Tippington School cast and crew on stage to take a bow. There was loud applause from the audience for all the schools that had taken part, especially for the winners, Mayfield School.

"It's a shame we didn't win," Rachel said to Kirsty, Tanya and Zac as they watched the Mayfield entrants take another bow. "But Mayfield School's *Aladdin* was really good. And I enjoyed putting on the play, didn't you, Kirsty?"

Kirsty nodded. "And best of all, nothing went wrong tonight because we got Leah's star back!" she whispered.

"I wonder what happened to Icy Towers School?" Zac remarked. "They didn't turn up to the auditions, did they?"

"It's strange, isn't it?" Tanya said, looking puzzled. "They seemed so keen this afternoon."

"Oh, perhaps they decided that the magic of the theatre just wasn't for them!" Rachel replied. And she winked secretly at Kirsty.

Now it's time for Kirsty and
Rachel to help...

Alesha the Acrobat Fairy

Read on for a sneak peek...

Bouncing Mad

"Wheeeeee!" squealed Kirsty Tate as she
whizzed down the helter-skelter, clinging
to the sides of the mat she was sitting
on. "Wheeee!" She was going faster
and faster as she shot around the bends,
her hair streaming out behind her in the
wind. Then she bumped down to a stop
at the end, and scrambled to her feet,
laughing...

Read **Alesha the Acrobat Fairy**
to find out what adventures are in store for
Kirsty and Rachel!

Meet the
Showtime Fairies

Collect them all to find out how Kirsty and
Rachel help their magical friends to save
the Tippington Variety Show!

www.rainbowmagicbooks.co.uk

Meet the
Friendship Fairies

When Jack Frost steals the Friendship Fairies' magical objects, BFFs everywhere are in trouble! Can Rachel and Kirsty help save the magic of friendship?

www.rainbowmagicbooks.co.uk

Calling all parents, carers and teachers!
The Rainbow Magic fairies are here to help
your child enter the magical world of reading.
Whatever reading stage they are at, there's
a Rainbow Magic book for everyone!
Here is Lydia the Reading Fairy's guide to
supporting your child's journey at all levels.

1

Starting Out
Our Rainbow Magic Beginner Readers are perfect for first-time readers who are just beginning to develop reading skills and confidence. Approved by teachers, they contain a full range of educational levelling, as well as lively full-colour illustrations.

2

Developing Readers
Rainbow Magic Early Readers contain longer stories and wider vocabulary for building stamina and growing confidence. These are adaptations of our most popular Rainbow Magic stories, specially developed for younger readers in conjunction with an Early Years reading consultant, with full-colour illustrations.

3

Going Solo
The Rainbow Magic chapter books – a mixture of series and one-off specials – contain accessible writing to encourage your child to venture into reading independently. These highly collectible and much-loved magical stories inspire a love of reading to last a lifetime.

www.rainbowmagicbooks.co.uk

"Rainbow Magic got my daughter reading chapter books. Great sparkly covers, cute fairies and traditional stories full of magic that she found impossible to put down" – Mother of Edie (6 years)

"Florence LOVES the Rainbow Magic books. She really enjoys reading now" – Mother of Florence (6 years)

The Rainbow Magic
Reading Challenge

Well done, fairy friend – you have completed the book!
This book was worth 5 points.

See how far you have climbed on the **Reading Rainbow**
on the Rainbow Magic website below.

The more books you read, the more points you will get,
and the closer you will be to becoming a Fairy Princess!

How to get your Reading Rainbow
1. Cut out the coin below
2. Go to the Rainbow Magic website
3. Download and print out your poster
4. Add your coin and climb up the Reading Rainbow!

There's all this and lots more at
www.rainbowmagicbooks.co.uk

You'll find activities, competitions, stories, a special
newsletter and complete profiles of all the
Rainbow Magic fairies. Find a fairy with your name!